...RY

JAMES

PERCY

MEET ALL THESE FRIENDS IN BUZZ BOOKS:

Thomas the Tank Engine
The Animals of Farthing Wood
Biker Mice from Mars
Winnie-the-Pooh
Fireman Sam
Rupert
Babar

First published in Great Britain 1995 by Buzz Books,
an imprint of Reed Children's Books
Michelin House, 81 Fulham Road, London SW3 6RB
and Auckland, Melbourne, Singapore and Toronto

ISBN 1 855 91496 4

Printed in Italy by Olivotto

TENDER ENGINES

buzz books

One morning, Gordon was in the yard taking on a large supply of coal.

"That's the third load of coal you've had today Gordon," said James. "Some might say you're being rather greedy."

"I'm an important engine," replied
Gordon. "Important engines need plenty of
coal but I doubt if you would understand
that James!"

James snorted and went about his work. Later, Gordon was taking on water from a standpipe because the water tower was under repair.

"I wouldn't drink too much of that water if I were you Gordon. It might give you boiler ache."

"Pah!" said Gordon. "What's this? Educating Gordon Day? First James and now you Duck. Big engines have big needs. Little engines are just annoying."

"Don't say I didn't warn you," laughed Duck.

Later, Gordon steamed into the yard at the Big Station.

"That's what I need," exclaimed Gordon.

There, emerging out of the sheds, were two shiny tenders.

12

"Now, if I had two tenders," said Gordon, "I wouldn't need to stop so often and I wouldn't have to listen to silly little engines."

"Those tenders belong to a visitor," replied his driver.

Diesel sidled up alongside.

"Everyone knows that tenders are a mark of distinction but I'm afraid that no amount of tenders will save you in the end. We diesels are taking over and we don't need tenders to make us important— not even one."

Gordon was most upset.

He was feeling just the same next day.

"I'm not happy."

"I know," put in Duck brightly. "It's boiler-ache."

"It's not boiler-ache," protested Gordon. "It's ... "

"Of course it is," interrupted Henry. "That water's bad. Your boiler must be full of sludge. Have a good wash-out. Then you'll feel a different engine."

"Don't be vulgar," huffed Gordon.

He backed down onto his train, hissing mournfully.

"Cheer up Gordon," said the Fat Controller.

"I can't, Sir. Is it true what Diesel says, Sir?"

"What does he say?"

"That diesels are taking over."

"Don't worry Gordon, that will never happen on my railway."

"One more thing, Sir. Why did the visitor have two tenders?"

"Because he lives on a railway with long distances between coaling depots."

Gordon felt better.

But Henry started complaining. He banged some trucks angrily.

"I always work hard enough for two," he puffed. "I deserve another tender."

Duck whispered something to Donald.
He was going to play a trick on Henry.
"Henry," he asked, "would you like my tenders?"
"Yours? What have you got to do with tenders?"

"All right," said Duck, "the deal's off.
Would you like them Donald?"

"I wouldna deprive you of the honour,"
replied Donald.

"It is a great honour," continued Duck
thoughtfully, "but I'm only a tank engine.
Perhaps James might ... "

"I'm sorry I was rude," said Henry hastily. "How many tenders have you, and when could I have them?"

"Err ... Ummmmm. I have six and you can have them this evening."

"Six lovely tenders," chortled Henry.
"What a splendid sight I'll be!"
Henry was excited all day.

"D'you think it will be all right?" he asked for the umpteenth time.

"Of course," said Duck. "They're all ready now."

The other engines waited where they
could each get a good view.

But Henry wasn't a splendid sight at all.
His six tenders were very old, dirty and
filled with boiler sludge!

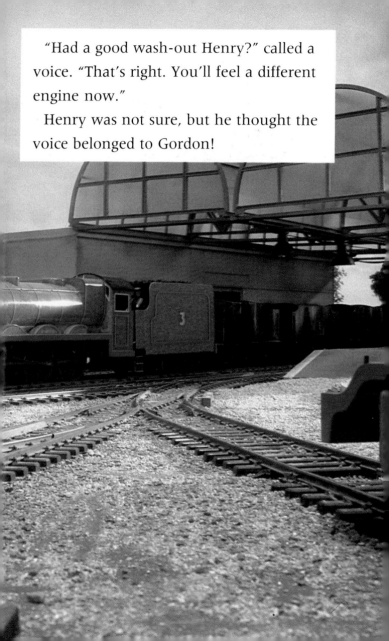

"Had a good wash-out Henry?" called a voice. "That's right. You'll feel a different engine now."

Henry was not sure, but he thought the voice belonged to Gordon!

THOMAS

EDWARD

GORDON